Everything Will Be Okay

A Poem about Dealing With Grief and Loss

DWANETTA BEAVER REED

Everything Will Be Okay: A Poem About Dealing with Grief and Loss

Copyright © 2024 by Dwanetta Beaver Reed
All rights reserved. This book or any portion thereof may not be reproduced or used in any manner whatsoever without the express written permission of the publisher except for the use of brief quotations in a book review.

Limits of Liability and Disclaimer of Warranty

The author and publisher shall not be liable for your misuse of this material. This book is strictly for informational purposes. The purpose of this book is to educate and entertain. The author and publisher do not guarantee anyone following these techniques, suggestions, tips, ideas, or strategies will become successful. The author and publisher shall have neither liability nor responsibility to anyone with respect to any loss or damage caused, or alleged to be caused, directly or indirectly by the information contained in this book. Views expressed in this publication do not necessarily reflect the views of the publisher.

Printed in the United States of America
Keen Vision Publishing, LLC
www.publishwithkvp.com
ISBN: 978-1-955316-75-0

In loving memory of my mother, Brenda Morrow Beaver.

A Message to Parents & Guardians,

Grief and loss are not happy topics to discuss. Unfortunately, both are experiences we cannot avoid. Tools, resources, and conversations surrounding grief and loss are necessary to help us navigate the challenges those experiences create. Loss covers a wide spectrum of circumstances, and this book, in particular, addresses the emotional whirlwind we experience when we lose loved ones.

When I was a child, I experienced the loss of relatives, but nothing prepared me for the year 2018. My seven-year-old daughter, Katherine, passed away, and my family and I were devastated. She left behind her five-year-old brother and a sister she asked for but never got to meet. As my husband and I grieved as parents, the greatest challenge was, and still is, comforting our grieving son.

Three years later, in 2021, my mother passed away. The pain of that loss penned the words of this book. One night, grief had me gripped, and I could not sleep. I reminded myself that holding in my emotions was not a healthy way of processing the pain. Once I allowed the tears and the words to flow, I soon found rest. I remembered that though we truly never get over losing those we hold dear, grief became easier to navigate after we allow ourselves to feel and release.

As adults, we often have an intimate, though undesired, relationship with grief and loss. Through life, we've learned to, at the very least, expect it to happen. Even if our methods may not be healthy, we've figured out some way to approach grief and loss. For children, however, grief and loss can be very confusing, frustrating, and overwhelming. Often, they don't understand what's happening or what the loss means. As parents and guardians, we may be so overwhelmed in our own grieving process that we forget children are navigating through the same loss, too. Therefore, this book has a dual purpose:

- To help children understand the emotions that come with loss and grief, and give parents and guardians a tool to discuss the thoughts, feelings, and emotions children may be experiencing.

- To encourage adults to also feel their feelings and find healthier ways to navigate the challenges of grief and loss.

I am not a therapist, but I offer this book to you and your family as one who intimately understands the grief journey.

This poem, *Everything Will Be Okay*, illustrates the experience of a family grieving the loss of a loved one. As the children grieve their grandmother, their parents grieve the loss of their mother. Together, they find a way to feel, process their emotions, hold on to old memories and create new memories that honor the woman they lost.

I pray this book helps you, your children, and your family find a path to healing. I encourage you and your children to express your emotions healthily together. That is where healing begins.

Dwanetta Beaver Reed

Lean into those feelings and give yourself grace...

Feel the sadness and the pain without too much haste.

Whatever you do, do not
hold those emotions in . . .

You don't want to explode, break down, or make your head spin.

Feel how you want and need to feel.
Take all the time you need to deal.

The best way to honor them is to keep on living.

Remember if they were here, they would want to see you smiling and grinning.

Know that you are loved in a special way.

You are important to this world every single day!

About the Author

Having developed a passion for reading at a young age, **Author Dwanetta Beaver Reed** dreamed of someday becoming a published author and writing children's books that promoted positive self-image and self-esteem. After Dwanetta's life took a devastating turn in 2018 when she and her husband lost their seven-year-old daughter, Katherine, she chose a different direction for her first publications. The challenge of comforting their son as he grappled with the loss of his older sister inspired Dwanetta to dedicate her first books to helping children navigate the challenges of grief and loss.

A devout Christian, Dwanetta considers her faith in and love for Jesus Christ the foundation of her life. She enjoys serving the community and volunteering as a Youth Leader at her church. Dwanetta is passionate about positively impacting the next generation and aims to make a difference in the lives of youth through every encounter she is granted.

By trade, Dwanetta is a systems engineer, having obtained a Bachelor's in Electrical Engineering from Tennessee State University and a Master's in Systems Engineering from the University of Alabama in Huntsville. However, she considers her most significant accomplishments being a wife, mother, daughter, sister, aunt, neice, cousin, and friend. Family and friends mean the world to Dwanetta, and she loves spending time with her loved ones, traveling, doing fun and new activities, and making lasting memories. Dwanetta wholeheartedly believes in being supportive, a great listener, and valuing relationships over monetary things. She hopes to instill these qualities in youth worldwide through books and other endeavors.

FACEBOOK Dwanetta Reed
INSTAGRAM @dwanetta51

Made in the USA
Columbia, SC
24 August 2024